Rachel is a first time author and after many years of writing as a hobby, she finally decided to take the plunge and have her writing published.

She is the proud mother of two strapping young lads, and you can also find her on TikTok (@crazycatlady) and Instagram (crazy cat lady official), where she shares photos of Lunar, her beloved cat and little ray of sunshine.

Rachel is a Fibromyalgia patient, and writing has been her salvation on many days, providing a welcome distraction from the chronic pain, fatigue, and other symptoms she experiences daily.

Jack and Mitchel both an inspiration to me,

your mom,

I love you both to the moon and back.

Rachel Barron

54 DAYS

AUSTIN MACAULEY PUBLISHERS™

LONDON • CAMBRIDGE • NEW YORK • SHARJAH

A CIP catalogue record for this title is available from the British Library.

ISBN 9781788486354 (Paperback)
ISBN 9781788486361 (ePub e-book)

www.austinmacauley.com

First Published 2023
Austin Macauley Publishers Ltd®
1 Canada Square
Canary Wharf
London
E14 5AA

Special thanks to all at Austin Macauley Publishers who had faith in my writing and took a chance on a first time author, I really appreciate all the hard work putting my book together and making it a reality. I will enjoy writing my second book knowing I have a huge support network behind me.

To both of my sons, Jack and Mitchell, you have been huge inspirations to my writing, helping with ideas and keeping me focused.

And to all of you lovely people who have purchased this copy and taken the time to read it, I really hope you enjoy reading this as much as I did writing it.

Chapter 1

It was six o'clock one June morning, the sun crept up into the highest point of the sky overlooking the quaint little road, cars gleaming in the sunlight, letterboxes awoken to the post arriving, blinds opened and the booms of trains flying past on the nearby rail track. The creaking of the bed stirred her from her sensual dream as she turned over fondly, holding the life-sized support pillow she often used to help her sleep thinking she was curled up next to the man who she's always loved but never told.

Angel glanced at the clock with squinted eyes just barely able to make out the time.

Hmmm, only 5 minutes till I have to face the world yet again! she reluctantly thought, and started drifting off.

Bleep...bleep...bleep... The alarm started screaming at her. 'Oh no,' she grunted, so she thumped on the snooze button with the palm of her hand and lay on her back staring up at the ceiling wondering what the day had in store. She could see the sun creeping through the crack in the curtains.

Angel Mayflower was a twenty-nine-year-old senior editor for a well-known publishing firm in the city of London and lived in an apartment on the border of town, Mews Road.

She lived there for five years after moving out of her parents' house.

Monday morning had arrived and yet again Angel felt so hung over and couldn't book another day off the limit had been reached; seemed she spent more time at home ill than she did at work and knew her boss would hit the roof! She lifted her head to see where her mobile phone was and felt like there was a lead weight attached and... *Wow!* the rush of pain that started thumping in her forehead was unbelievable, seems an army was on training day doing the conga in her eyeballs or so it felt. She didn't even manage to pick up the phone, all of a sudden a flushed feeling came over her like a wave in a tornado, mouthwatering, and she just knew what was about to happen next! She sat slumped on the floor whilst hugging the toilet after nearly not making it in time and thought to herself, *How did I get so selfish?* She must have snoozed off with her head laying on the rim of the toilet as what seemed only a few seconds was actually minutes and she was startled by the incessant beeping from the snooze on the alarm clock. *Great,* she huffed, slowly and carefully removed herself from the bathroom floor, stood up still feeling wobbly and turned the shower on. She paused for a moment catching a glimpse in the mirror, dark black rings under her eyes resembling shopping bags and a nice set of wrinkles appearing each side. Upon closer inspection, there was a line running down the middle of the mirror; she tutted and huffed at the thought of having to replace it even though it had been given to her as a gift. She wandered back into the bedroom to shut the alarm clock up and felt so dazed, she sat on the edge of the bed trying to wake herself up when out the corner of her eye she saw her mobile light up and flash. She reached over to see who it was and saw texts and missed calls from a mysterious number. Angel started to open and read the messages and drifted off into her own little world which wasn't hard to do. The landline started ringing; Angel jumped with fright, picked up the receiver as the phone was on the bedside table and answered with a tired cautious tone.

'Hello,' she muttered.

'Err…Hi…This is your knight in shining armour,' the voice said. She paused and had to think for a second, *Who?*

'Erm…Hello, do I know you?' she asked.

'Of course you do,' he said, and the line went dead. She paused again as her mind drew a total blank. Why was he saying this to her? Who was it? Her throat became very dry and she could feel her heart racing, and she started shaking and feeling very concerned as to what really happened on Saturday night. All sorts of images flashed round her mind like illuminations at a party. Her mobile phone lit up again and looked like it was dancing on the bedside table as it buzzed, only this time it was a memo reminder for a client whose work she had a deadline for which was today. Angel realised the time and left her phone on the bed and went to the bathroom to shower, her mind a sea of confusion. As she showered, lathering the soap all over her petite figure of a body, feeling the water run through her dark brown locks, she began to think of Saturday night. She put a firm foot down with herself as she needed to get ready to go to work and thought to herself, *I cannot face another reprimand from my boss for being late yet again.* She managed to get dressed and made herself look decent and smell nice, hair tied back into a ponytail, lipstick slapped on before giving a confident grin in the mirror. *Who am I kidding?* she sighed. Work bag – check;

phone – check; keys – check; handbag – check, and headed out of the door with seconds to spare.

Angel arrived into the office just in time and was relieved not to be late. She hadn't been sat down five minutes when the desk phone started to hum that annoying internal tune. *Oh no, I must be in trouble, it's the boss.* She nervously answered the call.

'Good morning, Mr Peg, how may I help you?

'Good morning, Angel, glad to hear you're on time this morning,' he said with a sarcastic tone.

'It seems your receptionist is the one late this morning.'

Angel didn't even register the comment, gulped and took a deep breath, he continued:

'Anyway, never mind that, I need a driver booking for midday, I have a very important meeting at Fletcher's. Do you think you could manage that?' still in his sarcastic tone.

Eyes rolled to the ceiling, she felt like answering with a very unprofessional reply, but her inner self put a brick wall up and somehow engaged her mouth to reply politely.

'Yes of course, sir, your driver will be here at midday as requested, I will do it now.' She could feel her teeth starting to clench together but still continued with the professional response.

'Anything else I can help you with?' she added.

'No, Angel, that will be all, for now.' She noted there was a very unfinished tone in his voice. She sat back in her office chair and let out a huge sigh, head still pounding from last night. She started to rummage around in the drawers of her desk and handbag, looking for some pain killers to help with her head and thought.

Coffee, I need coffee. She pressed the button to buzz the receptionist.

'Linda, can you bring me a strong coffee with two sugars, please?' she asked.

Some time had passed by and, odd, no answer from Linda or any sign of her coffee. She got up and made her way out to the receptionist's desk to see where Linda was.

Hmmm, no Linda? That's odd, she thought, *maybe she's gone off to do something.*

Angel heard footsteps coming up the corridor behind her and it was Jim, one of the senior accountants. He came into the kitchen area – he seemed OK.

'Morning, Angel,' he said.

'Oh, hi. Morning, Jim. Have you seen Linda this morning?' she asked with a puzzled expression on her face.

He paused for a moment and looked at Angel with sadness in his eyes, looked down at his mug and began to slowly stir his drink. Angel asked if he was OK.

'Have you not heard? Linda passed away at the weekend,' he replied quietly.

Completely flummoxed, Angel stood open-mouthed, completely stunned, she had no idea what to say to him. He told her that a mutual friend had contacted him that morning to let him know and if he could let Linda's work colleagues know. Suddenly, she wanted the floor to open up and swallow her whole. She didn't feel embarrassed at that moment but seemed she couldn't find the words to answer Jim. Her legs went weak, and she felt faint. Her face started to go warm with the slight embarrassment.

'Oh…oh…oh my god!' she exclaimed.

'How? Why? What happened?' she just about managed to get the words out. Jim shrugged his shoulders, said nothing and turned to walk away.

'Jim! I asked you a question! At least have the decency to bloody answer me!' she said with a raised tone in her voice.

'Angel, I don't know how or why,' he said.

Before another question could be asked, Jim very hastily walked off back to the direction of his office, coffee in hand. Angel stayed in the kitchen area completely bewildered and started to feel funny and then had a weird flashback from the weekend and very strangely seeing Linda in it!

After what felt like an eternity, Angel finally managed to get back to her desk and started to go into her own little world trying to digest the information that just passed her ears. Linda…dead? Surely not? It all seemed so surreal.

She was startled by the loud buzzing on the desk; it was her mobile, a text from her best friend, Helen. They had been best friends since high school.

It read, "Hi Hun, hope you're OK and recovered after the weekend? I have loads to tell you!! Lol, I know you're at work at Mo, so maybe we could meet l8r and have a cold one at Vino's? Anyways let me know ☺ xxx H xxx"

She sat staring at the text message, whole body numb, fingers frozen, not really knowing what to write. She eventually hit the reply button and started typing a message to Helen.

"Sure we can meet l8r… I have loads of questions??????… Say 8 pm at Vino's. Let's hope you have the answers I need! xxx A xxx"

She placed the phone back down on the desk and then suddenly realised a whole hour had passed and she still hadn't booked the driver for Pushy Peg. She reached down into the filing cabinet for the list of numbers connected with the company for a driver and phoned the first number at the top of the list.

'Good morning, Blue Stripes Cars, how may I help you?' a cheery voice said. Angel had heard this voice before and smirked.

'Ah...good morning. This is Miss Mayflower calling on behalf of Mr Alex Peg, CEO of Peggy Peg publishing house. I need to book a driver to pick Mr Peg up at 11.55 am promptly outside reception,' Angel said, feeling quite pleased with herself.

'Certainly, Miss Mayflower, I will have a driver there 11.55 am. Thank you for using Blue Stripes Cars, goodbye,' the voice said promptly. She replaced the receiver smiling to herself and then started to giggle like a school girl, and for a brief second or two, forgot the sad news she had previously received off Jim. She got up to actually go make a hot drink as she never got round to doing it. As she waited for the kettle to boil, she then started to think about poor Linda and what could have happened.

'Miss Mayflower?' Angel jumped with nervousness.

'Yes? Who called?' she said.

'Sorry, Miss Mayflower, I didn't mean to startle you.'

It was Peter, the maintenance man. He had come to have a look at the leaky radiator in her office and had got to the office earlier than planned.

'Oh, hello, Peter,' she said quietly. 'Sorry, I do apologise, my mind seems to be elsewhere today,' she said with an echo in her voice.

'Not a problem, Miss Mayflower,' he said with a pleasant smile.

'Oh, please call me Angel, Miss Mayflower sounds too formal,' she said as she returned the same polite smile, trying to look like all was fine.

'Sorry, Miss Mayflower—' he paused '—I mean Angel, I do believe you have a problem with your radiator in your office. Is it OK for me to go and have a look?' he asked eagerly.

She replied quietly, 'Yeah sure, knock yourself out.'

He went off to the office and Angel turned back to making her drink, only to find she hadn't even got herself a mug down let alone switched the kettle on to boil!

'Come on, girl, for god's sake!' she said out loud to herself, talk about needing to get a grip.

She looked up at the clock on the wall above the drinks station and it was 10.30 am already and she hadn't done anything other than book the car for the boss and yet she knew the deadline for one of the most important clients was due by end of the day! She made her drink and headed back to her office. Angel settled down at her desk, even though she had to contend with the noise of the banging from Peter fixing the radiator and fired up her computer, logged in and began to make a start. First stop, the dreaded email account, and as always there were so many.

'Hmmm…delete, delete, delete, delete, jeez, so many crap ones, why send them to me?! Good job this doesn't come through the post,' she sneered.

Angel found her eyes froze and was staring at the screen due to seeing an email from an unknown source, an email address she didn't recognize. She very gingerly pressed open and slowly began to read.

From: An Admirer
Date: 28th June
Subject: Saturday night
To: Angel Mayflower

To my darling Angel,
I so enjoyed our rendezvous Saturday night.
I do so wish for us to meet again and have a repeat of what we did.
I await your reply.
Yours forever,
XXXXX

Oh my, she found it hard to believe what she was reading, *this is bad, this is very bad!* she thought and panic started to set in. She sat back in her chair, her head buried deep into her hands. It was becoming obvious Angel and this mysterious guy must have had a one-night stand.

I know if I just ignore him, hopefully he will disappear, she thought.

So without any hesitation, she highlighted the email and hit the delete button as fast as she could, scrolled up to the settings options and blocked him from coming through to her email account.

Oh my, cannot believe that just happened! She just sat at her desk in disbelief.

She then started thinking about the text message received earlier from Helen, still wondering what the hell was going on

17

and what happened at the weekend and why. She started to drift off into a world of her own again, looked up at the windows in her office and saw people rushing around, but in slow motion? It lasted a few seconds till she realised the fire alarm was going off. *What the hell is going on now?!* she thought.

She ventured outside of the office into the reception area to see all the staff making their way towards the fire escape, footsteps that sounded like a stampede in a safari hurrying down the corridor. She stood frozen on the spot at her office door unable to move. The noise felt like it was getting louder as everyone proceed to go outside and she was no longer surrounded by people but very eerily on her own, still unable to move. Everything felt like it was still going in slow motion and she felt powerless to move her own body. The alarm had stopped but her ears were still ringing and felt like they were going to burst, trying to figure out what was happening, but nothing seemed to make any sense at all since she woke up this morning. *Am I dreaming?* she kept thinking to herself. She heard loud thumps getting closer to her location and was still frozen on the spot. She looked up and could just make out three figures in what looked like breathing masks and carrying large objects in their hands. One of the figures started to walk quickly towards Angel, shouting and waving their arms.

'Hey, are you OK, miss?' For a moment she couldn't find the words and her voice wouldn't work. She had to really muster the strength to squeak what sounded like garbage, 'Erm…yes…what is happening?' Suddenly, it all went pitch black and for a split second her body went all limp and lifeless.

Chapter 2

Arthur and his wife Rosaleen were doing their usual Monday routine in the garden. 'Such a beautiful day,' they both said and smiled at each other. They had been married for forty-nine years and made it look so easy. Angel was their only child and they were so proud of everything she had achieved in her life. Both were avid gardeners and lived a very simple life and took care of Angel's cat Lunar, who had to be left behind when Angel moved to the city due to a no pets policy in her apartment building. Lunar loved relaxing in the garden with Arthur and Rosaleen, laying on her back, basking in the hot sun as she did on many occasions when she wasn't trying to chase the birds. Lunar had been with the Mayflowers since she was eight weeks old and had such a funny little character, which is why it broke Angel's heart to leave her behind but knew she would be looked after so well by her parents.

Rosaleen was knelt down replanting new bulbs in her immaculate flowerbed when out of the corner of her eye she saw Lunar playing with one of the new flower pots, flinging it up in the air and chasing it. *Daft cat,* she thought smiling to herself.

It brought back memories of when Angel was a young child and they had their other cat Charlie, who used to play with everything and anything except the cat toys he was given. When the phone rang, she shouted to Arthur to answer it, but he never answered her so she got up and went inside the house.

'Hello – Chepstow 5467834,' she said cheerfully.

'Hello, may I speak with Mr or Mrs Mayflower please?' a male voice replied.

'This is Mrs Mayflower speaking, may I ask who is calling?' she replied with a slight tone of worry.

The male voice continued, 'This is Dr Cote, I am one of the senior consultants at St Dermal's Hospital in London and I need to speak with you and your husband regarding your daughter Angel Mayflower,' he paused. 'She's been involved in an accident,' he said and Rosaleen gasped. She wasted no time with details and told the doctor they would be there. Somewhat shocked and confused, Rosaleen needed to speak with Arthur but strangely didn't know where he was. She saw Arthur had left his mobile phone in the kitchen on the table so had no way of contacting him. She went upstairs to pack a bag as she knew they would probably be staying a couple of nights.

She kept saying to herself, 'It won't be that bad, Angel has more than likely just had a fall or something and has had to stay in hospital. The doctor didn't seem too concerned on the phone.'

The house phone rang again and this time it was Arthur. He told Rosaleen he had popped down the road to the garden centre and whilst in there bumped into their nephew Billy, decided to go back to Billy's house for a cuppa hence the phone call. Rosaleen told Arthur about the call from the doctor. Arthur wasted no time in driving back home. Before he left, he asked Billy if he would mind looking after Lunar for a few days. Arthur and Rosaleen sorted a few things out, packed their bags and started their journey from Chepstow to London to see their little girl who was always nicknamed Daisy as a child.

The journey felt like it was never going to end, cars galore, lorries rushing past them on the motorway. A strange black cloud descended over them and it rained heavily as if out of nowhere, the wipers on the car working overtime, *swish, swoosh, swish, swoosh*. Arthur kept seeing delay signs on the overhead gantry which in secret filled him with dread as neither of them knew the extent of how bad Angel was or how she had been injured, but for the sake his wife he kept smiling and reassuring her that all was going to be fine, or so he hoped.

Angel found herself waking up in the hospital surrounded by a doctor and two nurses, and she just lay on the bed staring up at the ceiling not being able to reply or make any kind of movement to indicate she understood anything, even though she could hear every noise going on in the ward.

The nurse on duty was at her bedside taking her blood pressure and checking her oxygen levels. She looked at Angel and just smiled; Angel just looked back at her with a blank expression and then looked away again feeling a hot tear fall down her cheek. The nurse spoke to Angel with a soft tone and asked if she was feeling OK or was in any pain. Angel decided she wouldn't be getting those Paracetamols again due to the fact they hadn't worked, as her head was pounding more than ever now. Angel still couldn't look at the nurse so just shook her head so the nurse would go away.

Angel's eyelids banged down feeling like lead weights and it seemed to take forever for them to retract open again, her mind such a massive blur, and she felt like a massive fog had descended over her.

The doctor appeared at her bedside and said, 'Good afternoon, Angel, how are you feeling?'

She raised one eyebrow at him as if to say, 'How the hell do you think I feel?!' He started to check her blood pressure which annoyed Angel considering the nurse had not long checked it and started talking about something to do with her office and a brick landing on her head – A WHAT?! She squeezed his hand tightly so he had to look at her directly and she tried so hard to croak to him quietly, but instead gave a big cough, cleared her throat and bellowed to him:

'I will ask you once and once only,' she took a deep breath. 'What the flipping hell has happened and where am I?' He took a deep sigh and a small step away from her to pull the chair next to her bed closer and sat down next to her.

He looked at her and said, 'From what we were told by the ambulance staff that brought you here, apparently part of the office building caught fire and a wall collapsed. They think you were trapped in the smoke for a while and it caused you to pass out, and just as you hit the floor, you landed on your side then a brick fell and landed on the back of your head.'

'Oh,' she replied, feeling strange, then all of a sudden, like a monsoon, the thoughts and memories of that weekend came flooding back, invading her brain, causing flashbacks of which contained information to do with.

'Oh my god....'

'It can't be...'

'No she isn't…'

'Linda!!'

Hot streams of tears either side of her face came crashing down her cheeks like big boulders off a mountain, her friend Linda in her mind, having a ball, as the girls did on many weekends, but this was no normal weekend.

Angel shouted over to the nurse's station, and a very stern looking nurse marched over. 'We'll have no shouting on this ward. If you want one of us, you will have to push your buzzer like all the other patients and wait your turn!' And she walked off!

Bloody charming! Angel thought. *So what now? I know I will get out of bed and go and find someone myself.*

With some discomfort and difficulty, she managed to sit up and swing her legs round so they dangled freely on the side of the bed, looked down at the floor and saw what looked like a handbag half hanging out of the locker next to the bed.

Hmmm, weird, how did my handbag get here? she thought.

'I'm sure I left you under my desk?' she muttered out loud. The patient in the next bed started looking over. Angel was driving herself mad not being able to put details of that weekend together and today's events together in a logical order, whilst also trying to piece together the catastrophe at work that had landed her in hospital.

A tune started echoing down the corridor towards the ward which made Angel smile. It was getting louder and nearer, and round the corner two very familiar faces appeared. 'MOM! DAD!' she shrieked!

Angel was really shocked to see her parents but at the same time so relieved as finally something made sense of this stupid day. She slid her painful body down towards the floor and managed to hook the bag onto her foot and lifted it up enough for Arthur to bend down and grab her bag.

He said in a soft tone, 'You rest, my Daisy-Doo.' He hadn't called Angel that name since she was a little girl. She opened her bag to find her mobile phone as she was eager to send a message to Helen. She tried to switch the phone on but seems it had no battery life left in it so asked her dad Arthur if he could go and ask one of the nurses if a charger was available. Her dad went off in search at his daughter's request, which gave Angel and her mom a few minutes to talk.

She shoved her phone under the pillow, as the last thing she wanted was the phone confiscated, although having her dad go and ask for a charger kind of gave the game away. She swung her legs back on to the bed and was enjoying a relaxing conversation with her mom which for the first time that day felt completely normal.

'I've found one,' her dad said.

Arthur returned looking very pleased. He'd managed to obtain a charger just on loan from one of the health care assistants. Angel couldn't get her phone plugged in quick enough.

'Slow down, love,' Arthur said, 'what's the hurry with charging your phone?' He sounded a bit put out, considering he and Rósaleen had travelled miles to come and visit. Angel looked at him for a moment and then broke down in tears.

'Dad, you have no idea what I have been through today!' she sobbed.

Arthur looked at his wife and then back at Angel and apologised for sounding rude.

The bell started ringing to indicate visiting time was over and Angel's parents got up and said goodbye to their daughter, kissed her on the cheek and promised to return the next day. Angel nodded in between tears and blew them a kiss. The phone had been charging for a good twenty minutes when it started buzzing round the cabinet top. Angel's attention soon went off her tears and onto her phone. She very subtly started to read the texts coming through; one was from Helen.

"Angel as soon as you get this text me ASAP!!!

xxx H xxx"

Through blurred eyes, as her head was still pounding, made even worse from crying earlier on, she managed to find the reply button.

"Helen, I'm in the hospital, alive, or at least just about! If you have any answers on Linda, please tell me. I'm in St Dermal Hospital, Ward 24; visiting times not sure, please come and see me ASAP! Please hinnies, I need some answers.

xxx A xxx"

Angel stared at the screen kind of half expecting an answer straight away but closed the phone shut and waited for a reply. She had an awful feeling in the pit of her stomach, a feeling she always got when something horrible had happened and it was really scary.

Chapter 3

Visiting time arrived the next day and the other patients had their family and friends around them, and Angel saw a familiar face walking towards her bed.

Ah, it's Helen. She sighed in relief, secretly keeping fingers crossed she had good news.

'Hi mate,' Helen said.

She seemed in a very jolly mood.

'Hey Hells,' Angel replied.

'How are you feeling?' Helen asked with a relieved look on her face, 'You took a nasty bump to the head, so I heard?'

Angel looked at Helen very sternly, almost the same way the nurse did previously.

'I really don't care about my head at present, Helen,' she said, 'I need to discuss an important matter with you.' There was an awkward pause from both ladies. Angel looked at Helen like she had seen a ghost.

'What's up, Angel?' she asked.

Angel started to get suspicious from the shifty look on Helen's face but decided to proceed anyway with the burning desire to find out the truth.

'Remember the weekend just gone, Helen?' she asked assertively.

'Yes I do,' Helen paused 'but would rather forget it,' she sighed.

Helen seemed less than excited from her reply. Angel narrowed her eyebrows close together and had a somewhat serious expression.

'Erm, well, I couldn't remember the details this morning,' Angel blurted out, 'and erm, well, now I can. Seems the bump on the head has done me the world of good and I can remember every detail from Saturday night.'

Helen gulped loudly. 'Oh, really?' she replied hesitantly.

'Yes, really!' Angel snapped back. She could tell Helen was hiding something and it was becoming obvious she wanted to refrain from spilling the beans.

'So come on then, Helen,' she took a slight pause, 'you obviously know something, so please don't hold back.'

Angel was starting to get really impatient and knew time was running out and that any moment the bell could go indicating visiting time over.

'Come on then what?' Helen sarcastically replied, messing about in her pockets, in fact doing anything else but look at Angel.

'Helen, tell me what happened Saturday night,' she calmly said.

Angel spoke each word slowly ensuring she would hear. Helen looked at her in such a distant manner, almost like she was looking through a window.

'I don't, I can't, and oh, Angel, just leave it please! For your sake!' she bellowed.

'I will not leave it!' Angel snapped again. 'And what do you mean for my sake, Helen?' she said angrily. By this time

Angel could feel her whole body getting tense, sensing Helen wanted to say more but was choosing to keep quiet. *Ding.*

'Oh bloody hell, there's the damn bell,' Angel muttered to herself quietly.

Helen very swiftly got up from the bed and went to walk away, and looked back at Angel.

'Excuse me, Helen, where do you think you're going?' Angel asked quickly whilst Helen was trying to hurry out of the ward.

'The visiting times are over and I have to go… Erm, bye Angel, get well soon,' her voice echoed as she scurried out.

But before another word could be said all, Angel could do was watch Helen walk quickly back down the corridor and then she was gone.

She gave out a huge sigh and sat for a few minutes going over what seemed a really pointless conversation. She decided the best way to keep any information fresh was to write it all down. Even though her eyes were still slightly blurred, she had to try. She called for the nurse.

'Yes, my dear, how can I be of help?' the nurse asked. It was Maxine, one of the auxiliary nurses.

'Hi, Maxine, I was wondering if you could get me a piece of paper and a pen? It's really urgent, I need to write some important information down!'

Maxine looked at Angel quite concerned. 'Are you OK, my love? Anything you want to talk about? I am about to go on a break if you fancy a chat, confidentially of course,' she said, stood with her hands clasped in front of her and smiled.

Angel just smiled back at her and put on a brave face so as to try to not arouse suspicion.

'Erm, thanks, Maxine, but I'm OK. I just need to write some stuff down before I forget again.'

Angel tried to make it humorous so Maxine would back off. *Why the hell would I want some woman I know nothing about to come and sit on my bed and have a lovely cosy chat? Aft! Don't think so!'* she thought. Her cage was rattled enough after the disaster conversation with Helen.

Maxine went off to the nurse's station to fetch the paper and pen and returned within a few minutes.

'One piece of paper and a pen,' Maxine said with a smile and popped it down on the hospital table.

'Thank you, Maxine,' Angel said with a smile.

'No problem, hinnies,' Maxine said with a wink.

Hmmm ok... she paused for a moment, *either I am being over sensitive or she just winked at me?* Angel thought and with a shake of her head, put the wink to the back of her mind and settled in bed pulling the hospital table up towards her and got on with putting Saturday night back together once and for all in logical order.

Chapter 4

"Saturday 26th July

Night out with myself, Helen, Linda

Finished work at 1pm, Linda came home with me and Helen came round later around 5pm.

I cooked us a meal first, to go out on a lined stomach very important I told the girls, as I knew how much alcohol would be consumed.

Meal consisted of a quick cheesy pasta bake and garlic bread, plenty of carbs to soak up the drink.

Bottle of white wine and some music to get us in the party mood. Helen and Linda went upstairs to get ready while I washed and tidied up.

Helen then shouted down that the bathroom was free so I put the plates and everything away and made my way upstairs. I then went into my bedroom and started looking through my wardrobe for an outfit, decided to wear my gold dress, not too revealing, and put my matching gold shrug on as the weather was a bit cool, with my golden heeled shoes.

8pm and the taxi arrived and we got into the taxi and headed into town, first stop being Vino's, our favourite wine bar. We didn't stay long, had one drink and then proceeded to make our way around the bars with the plan to end up at Fab Five disco bar on the high street."

'Oh my god!' she gasped and stopped writing. Sat in her hospital bed, her mind started to re-live the events that occurred when the girls arrived at Fab Five, hands started to shake as her mind played the images one after another. 'Now I am scared,' she said to herself quietly. She took a deep breath and carried on writing.

"There wasn't many in Fab Five at first but we arrived at 11pm so still plenty of time. I remember Helen went off to the loo and seemed to take ages but me and Linda both made our way through to the outside smoking hut and both lit up a cigarette chatting about general stuff. After a while I noticed a man who kept looking over and smiling. Our eyes met and he then came over and asked for a light. Linda's eyes lit up with excitement and gave this man a light for his smoke. He introduced himself as Steve."

'Flipping heck, I remember now!' she exclaimed, 'Steve spoke to Linda first!'

Forgetting where she was, she looked up and saw the other patients looking over; seems she had verbalised her thoughts out loud and everyone could hear what she was saying to herself.

'Oops, sorry, think I said that a tad loud,' she said feeling a little on the embarrassed side.

The woman opposite asked if all was OK, and the woman to her left gave such a sharp look, to be honest, if looks could kill…

Angel replied to the woman opposite whilst feeling rather warm in the cheeks, 'Yes, I'm OK, thanks, just trying to recall the weekend's events, memory is a little rusty,' she said, which after all that had happened, being a little rusty was an understatement.

'Anything I can help with?' the lady asked.

'Erm, well, unless, erm, in fact, I'm OK thanks,' Angel hesitantly replied with a sort of a smile that looked more like an awkward smirk.

She needed to carry on writing and get all this information out of her head, as it felt like her brain was about to explode, so she picked up the pen and her hand seemed to just go off on its own, writing letters that were forming into words and Angel felt no control but was transfixed on the sentences developing.

"Helen finally came back from the loo looking rather flushed ☺ and me and Linda just giggled. We introduced Steve to Helen and she blushed as she shook his hand. I noticed the chemistry between them straight away and the look they both gave each other, and I asked if they already knew each other; they did, in fact, he was the reason she was so long in the loo. Steve went off to the bar and I pulled Helen to a quiet corner to get all the dish details.

I didn't need to ask too many questions as it soon became obvious what had happened.

The night then carried on with Steve starting to flirt with me and Linda on the dance floor, and he brought us many drinks. I squinted at my watch at one point and could just make out the time 1:07am I was very drunk and couldn't seem to think straight. I remember feeling very sick and went off to the loo. Linda found me sitting on the floor feeling very sorry for myself and I asked her where Helen was and she didn't know, she thought she was with me in the loo.

I reached into my bag for my phone, but couldn't find it. I emptied my bag and it was gone which worried me as I never lose my phone.

I asked Linda to text Helen or call and see where she was. She did and had no reply. We both started to get worried. I got up best I could and felt dizzy, my vision a little blurred, but I put that down to the drink. We made it out the loo and scouted the club for Helen but there was no sign of her.

After a good half hour, we both decided she must've met a bloke but then we noticed there was no sign of Steve either, so we thought she had gone home with him, but strange how she didn't tell us though. Whilst we sat trying to sober up, the DJ called my name across the mic to go to him straight away. My first thought was Helen had come back and couldn't find us but it wasn't, my phone had been found. The person who had it, handed it in with strict instructions to the DJ to not to call me to the booth until exactly 1:45am. I looked at my watch and it was exactly that time. I rushed back to Linda who was enjoying the company of a guy! I remember he kept staring at me in a funny way and I asked Linda to have a word but with the combination of drink and music, she said to stop being paranoid. We walked out of Fab Five at 3:00am and there were a high number of police cars and officers around, which wasn't unusual as normally there is a punch-up or fight. I decided to walk home to try and clear my head. Linda and the guy she met walked the other way, the guy seemed eager to get Linda away on her own. With me being drunk, I assumed he wanted to have his way with her, after all she did say before we went out she wanted to pull and hopefully have sex with a guy, so who was I to interfere."

Tears started streaming down Angel's face and the ink was starting to run on the page because of her tears dropping onto the paper. She put the pen down and threw her hands into her face and started to sob heavily. The woman in the bed opposite saw her sobbing and called for the nurse to come over.

Maxine approached the bed. 'Angel, everything OK?' she asked softly.

In between sobs, she replied, 'No it's not!' *Sob*. 'I hate myself!'

Angel was heartbroken as the full realisation had hit her like a freight train ploughing into a brick wall at full speed!

The nurse perched herself on the end of the bed and asked if Angel would like to go somewhere private to have a chat, as clearly she had something she needed to get off her chest. She nodded and got out of bed.

Chapter 5

Angel dried her tears and found herself sitting in a lovely office wondering who was going to walk in. She noticed the lovely artwork on the wall, an array of pink and peach subtly mixed together, almost how the sky looks on a summer's morning just before the sun comes up. The door opened, taking her attention off the artwork, and her eyes were immediately brought to attention of a man entering the office; quite tall, blonde wavy hair, and a blue pin-stripe suit with a crisp white shirt finished with an exquisite pale blue tie, immaculately knotted at the top button, very neatly attired. He opened his jacket button and sat down at the desk.

'Hello, Angel, my name is Dr Cote, I'm one of the resident consultants here at St Dermal,' he took a slight breath, 'One of the nurses looking after you has asked me to have an informal chat with you, is that OK?' he asked with a formal tone which did not sit well with Angel. She stared at him with a blank expression thinking to herself, *Do the nurses think I am going insane?* She paused for a second.

'I'm not mad,' she told him with a miffed expression.

'Nobody is saying you are, Angel,' he replied with a smile, 'but you have been showing signs of erratic behaviour,' he said.

'Erratic?!' she snapped. She stared at him with wide eyes, almost like the devil trying to remove someone's soul. He pulled his lips together and took a big sigh.

'OK, listen, maybe erratic was the wrong word to use,' he replied.

'You're damn right it's the wrong word,' she said angrily. She took a deep breath and decided to tell him what she knew.

'I have had a series of events happen in the last few days that I have been trying to make sense of and it's only since being admitted here I have been able to remember everything in the correct order and have started to write it down,' she paused quickly and realised she had come without the paper.

'Erm, I need to go back to the ward, there is something I have forgotten,' she said with a slight panicked tone in her voice. She got up to make her way towards the door when Dr Cote held up a screwed-up bit of paper with scribbled notes on.

'Is this the paper?' he asked.

'Yes, oh my god, you have it!' she gasped in relief, not even wondering how he came to have it, and she sat back down.

'Angel,' he said, 'take a deep breath and tell me in your own words what has been happening and let's see if we can get to the bottom of it?' he seemed genuinely concerned for her, but she felt so stupid and was beginning to think it was a pointless exercise.

She looked him straight between the eyes. 'Why don't you read my notes!' she said with a sarcastic tone.

The doctor gave her a blank expression, took his glasses out of his crisp pocket and started to read the notes. She sat twiddling her thumbs, fidgeting in general, stared at the ceiling, started humming a tune, scratched her head, and it seemed like ages. He eventually finished, calmly took his glasses off, crossed his legs, put his elbow on his leg with his chin cup in his hand and had what looked like a very patronising look on his face and said just two words:

'Good story,' he smirked slightly.

'Story?!' she gasped in disbelief.

'Yes,' he said calmly.

'Story?! I'll give you story!' she snapped angrily. Angel stood up and pushed the chair back and raised her voice. She could feel herself getting so worked up.

She took yet another deep breath and said, 'This is not a story, it's the events that happened to me and two of my best friends when we went out on Saturday night, and now one of my best friends is dead! She could feel the tears welling up in her face and her throat felt like a frog had taken up residence.

His eyes widened and he uncrossed his legs, pulled himself closer to the desk, looking puzzled.

'Dead?' he said in a shocked and soft tone.

'Yes, dead – 'D E A D!' she snapped again angrily.

This time the tears escaped from her tear ducts and started running down her cheeks, feeling like streaks of hot water on her face.

She managed to squeeze a few words in a breath, 'Which part of dead do you not understand?' She looked at him sternly. 'Come on, tell me, you're the doctor!'

By now she was so riled with anger and wasted no time standing up in his office and started pacing up and down his neatly fitted carpet, ruffling the matching shag pile rug, waving her arms around. She was mad, mad, mad!

'I am very sorry for your loss, Angel,' he replied with a sort of sympathetic tone. 'Let's talk about it?' he added.

'I don't want to bloody talk! I want answers. I want to know what's happened to my best friend Linda!

She fell in a heap on the floor and started sobbing again to herself.

'Why did this have to happen? Why is it happening to me? I hate myself, I hate myself, I hate myself! It's all my fault, it's all my fault!' she continued.

The phone rang in his office. 'I am sorry, Angel, I need to excuse myself as I am on duty, please feel free to sit here as long as you need to, I will pop by the ward later to see how you are,' he said and left his office.

Bloody great! she thought.

After ten minutes or so of staring into nowhere and biting on her nails, she decided to go back to the ward. She took one more look at the artwork on the wall and smiled, then left the doctor's office. On her way back up the corridor, Angel saw a sign on the wall; it read: "Hospital Chapel". She stopped for a moment and stood staring at the sign and all she could think of was Linda. She made her way towards the chapel and felt like it was her duty to say a prayer for her best friend, the best friend she grew up with and went to school with, shared make-up tips with.

Once inside, it was very silent, no sound from anywhere, even a pin dropping would have been loud, it was that quiet. The room glowed and shadows flickered on the walls from the display of candles that had been previously lit, obviously by other relatives or even other patients. Angel walked slowly towards them. She lit a candle and said the name Linda privately to herself. The wick glowed as it connected with the lighting stick and made a calm flame flickering slightly. She closed her eyes and mimicked a cross by hand on her chest and said a little prayer.

'Linda, I love you and will never forget you. You're my best friend and always will be. We had some amazing times and I hope you're in a better place. I promise I will find out the truth about what happened to you and will bring down whoever is responsible.'

Angel sat quiet and seemed to get swept up in the moment. The door opened to the chapel and made Angel jump.

'Oh sorry, I didn't realise anyone was in here,' said a voice from behind the door.

It was the hospital priest. She just gave him a blank look and said, 'No, it's OK, in fact I was just leaving.'

She turned around and walked towards the door and walked past the priest without a second glance, she headed back to the ward in a complete daze.

Back at the bed, she just sat and stared at the floor. In the background she could hear the trolleys getting closer. Looking up at the clock to see it was 5:00 pm, dinner time, and for some strange reason, she remembered that the doctor broke his promise about coming back to the ward to see her. She could hear the catering staff in the bay and a very tall skinny young lad came to her bed.

'Do you want pie or sausage?' he bellowed.

She turned her head and raised an eyebrow, not overly impressed with being spoken to like that. 'Pardon?' she asked.

He repeated the question with an impatient tone of voice. Still raising an eyebrow, Angel gave him a deep meaningful miffed expression and returned the sarcastic tone:

'I heard you the first time. Is that anyway to speak to a patient?' she said.

He huffed and looked straight at her. 'Listen, bird, I have got loads peeps to get fed, I ain't got time for no messing,' he said with one hand impatiently on his waist.

Angel looked straight at him and all of a sudden started laughing.

What is this language I'm hearing? she thought, *Jeez, takes me back to when I was young,* and laughed again. She quickly realised he was only doing his job and what he said wasn't really important so she answered him, 'OK mate, I will have pie please,' she said.

'One pie and mash,' he hastily replied, plonked it on the table and moved onto the next bed. Half an hour went by and the pie and mash was still sat where it was plonked, getting colder by the minute. Angel's appetite had hibernated and refused to resurface; even though her belly was actually rumbling slightly, she just couldn't face any food and the smell was making her feel a little queasy.

The lady in the bed opposite had noticed nothing had been touched and kindly said to Angel, 'You must eat to keep your strength up, sweetie.'

Angel smiled. 'I know, I'm just not hungry,' she said with a bit of a screwed-up face. She heard the squeaky wheels of the trolleys coming back, a voice behind her brought a smile even though she felt so depressed.

'Yaw bird, I don't believe it, after all the gabbing, yaw did still ain't polished grub!' followed by a big huff. She turned and looked with a muddled expression as to why this young lad would care about whether she ate her food or not. He is getting paid to serve the meals whether eaten or not, so why would he care.

He walked off muttering, 'Bloody wasters,' under his breath.

Angel took slight offence to his comment and felt she had to speak up, 'I beg your pardon, mate? Do you want to say that a bit louder so we all can hear you?'

He never replied and walked off, slightly turning a nice shade of red. The lady opposite just smiled and nodded as if to say well done.

Chapter 6

A whole week had flown by and Angel was getting proper itchy feet being stuck in the hospital as she put it.

'Come on, wake up,' a female voice hollowed, as she was rudely awoken.

Her eyes opened briefly, only to hear the voice of the matron, or Dragon as Angel named her.

'Good morning, Angel,' she chirped.

Angel groaned a kind of sound that sort of resembled morning to her and muttered under her breath for the old bat to go away and leave her to sleep. She reached for her phone off the bed cabinet to see the time, her head slammed back into the pillow.

'Oh my god, are you serious?!' she muttered to herself.

It said 7:02 am. She felt even more depressed. The one place where people are supposed to rest and it felt like a military camp being woken up at 7 am.

The dragon finished faffing around and said to her, 'I will be back in ten minutes, Angel. Doctor wants a blood sample from you,' and walked off smiling.

Angel rolled her eyes and huffed, 'Oh lovely, what a way to wake up, all heart you are!'

The old bat stopped in her tracks, turned, looked at her sternly, 'I will have you know, madam, I have a heart of gold,' she replied.

Angel let out a snigger and pulled the covers up to her face and felt like a naughty child and without thinking cheekily threw a response, 'Yeah, and so does a hardboiled egg.' The matron looked perplexed.

Angel couldn't stop sniggering.

A few minutes later, as promised, the doctor made his way to the bedside, pushing a little table in front of him and on it was the biggest needle she had ever seen in her life, which kind of made it the second, as the last needle was way back at high school after her childhood injections.

Angel thought to herself, *We won't go there*, and smirked.

'Good morning, Angel, I am Dr Glover. I trust the nurse has told you we need to take some blood?'

She nodded and looked at him warily wondering exactly how much blood he wanted; the size of the needle made her want to vomit. She paused for a moment.

'Why do you need to take blood?' she asked nervously.

He smiled and replied, 'We just need to run a few tests.'

Angel wasn't having any of it and started to get argumentative. 'B… b…but I had tests a few days ago, so I don't need any more blood taken, thank you very much!'

By this time now, she was wide awake and very suspicious. The doctor perched on the end of the bed.

'Yes, I'm aware of your tests from the doctor who assessed you on your admission. Thing is, the results were inconclusive, so we need to do them again so we can compare the results,' he replied.

She still wasn't happy, she asked for a second opinion, also to see the results of the last lot of tests, not that she would be able to understand the results, but there was something about this doctor she couldn't put her finger on, and just didn't trust him, that she knew for sure he looked at her surprised by the request.

'Oh, OK,' he replied.

She stood her ground as a patient and he had to respect her wishes. He then stood up, nodded in relation to her statement and informed her he would arrange for his colleague to come and have a chat later on. She thanked him and he returned to the main desk.

She took a deep breath and decided to get dressed and go for a walk outside around the hospital grounds, thinking the fresh air might make her feel a bit better as she still felt queasy. She realised she hadn't asked anyone to bring in any personal items and was about to press the call button when down on the chair there were clean clothes and her own wash bag. *That's Mom and Dad,* she thought and smiled. Without any haste, she had a refreshing wash and put her clothes on, made her way back to the bed, put her things away and was about to put her shoes on when a voice behind her made her smile.

'Hello beautiful,' the voice said.

Angel turned around slowly, trying to hide the excitement that felt like a firework about to explode.

'Dad!' she shrieked.

For the first time in over a week, Angel felt completely safe. This was the only man in her life she had 100% trust and faith in, and she couldn't believe he was there, now, standing in front of her even though he'd been before with her mom.

He'd phoned up beforehand and asked permission to visit outside of visiting hours.

He said nothing and just smiled. She fell into his arms and started to cry. Feeling his arms wrapping around her was so comforting. He pulled her in close and said everything was going to be OK. Her cheeks felt very hot as tears started to fall again. She looked up into his eyes. He reached into his pocket for a tissue and wiped both eyes gently.

'Don't cry, sweetheart, I'm here now,' he said softly.

'I'm overwhelmed to see you, Dad!' Angel whimpered.

She put her hand over his hand on her cheek and composed herself enough to ask if he wanted to join her for a walk in the grounds. He nodded with excitement.

'You try stopping me, love,' he replied.

Angel sat down on the chair next to the bed and couldn't put her shoes on fast enough. They both walked down the ward towards the door hand in hand, father and daughter.

They headed out onto the main corridor and decided to walk down the two flights of stairs instead of taking the lift. Arthur couldn't stop smiling and squeezing his beautiful daughter's hand. As nice as it was, she couldn't help noticing something wasn't right. Heading outside, they turned left away from the car park and walked along the path towards the little flower garden within the hospital grounds, stopped near the little stream and sat on the bench. Angel looked at Arthur with concern.

'Are you OK, Dad?' she asked.

He looked at her surprised. 'Yes, my darling, couldn't be better. Why do you ask?' he tried to sound genuine.

'No reason,' she replied, still trying to work out why she could still sense a negative atmosphere. She asked again, 'You don't seem yourself, Dad? Please tell me what's wrong.'

He still wouldn't say a word so she decided to change the subject slightly. 'How's Uncle Bert doing? she asked with a slight more cheer in her voice, 'I heard from Cousin Billy a couple of months ago, he said Uncle Bert had gone off to live in America.'

Arthur looked at Angel and let out a big sigh. 'As far as I know, he is OK, making big bucks, 'you know what your Uncle Bert is like, money mad!' he said.

Arthur was still distracted. It was starting to irritate Angel. Her dad had never been like this before, always such an open person normally and yet he wouldn't share the information with her, his only daughter. She turned to face him whilst still sat on the bench and clasped his hands with her hands, looking deep into his eyes.

'Dad, I'm your daughter and I love you unconditionally. Whatever is troubling you, we can overcome it together!'

A small tear rolled down his cheek and he bowed his chin for a brief moment, then lifted his head and looked at Angel in an emotional way she had never seen from him before.

'My darling Angel, you have enough to be dealing with at the moment, I really shouldn't say anything,' he paused, took a very big deep breath and continued, 'your mom told me not to tell you yet.'

Angel listened attentively as the once very proud man she remembered as a little girl was sat in front of her reduced to tears. *What could be troubling him so much that he couldn't talk to me?* she thought.

'Please, Dad, tell me I need to know,' she asked softly. She felt her heart start to pound as he lifted his head again, cleared his throat and dropped the biggest bombshell.

Chapter 7

She waited patiently whilst her dad struggled to get his words out.

'Angel, my beautiful daughter, you are the only thing in my life that I'm very proud of but...' he paused.

'But what?' she said softly.

He looked at Angel with sorrowed eyes. 'Promise you will not hate me for what I'm about to say?' he said, and she nodded.

'I promise, Dad. I love you, I told you that,' she said softly.

He took a deep breath and carried on, 'OK, the person responsible for your best friend's death has been caught by the police and is being questioned.'

'What?!' she gasped 'How? Who?'

She could feel her head filling up with many questions and her emotions were starting to whirl round her body like a tornado at its worst. She struggled to digest the words and started to cry.

Arthur tilted his head to one side and lifted his hand and started to push her hair behind her ear, the same way he did when she was a little girl and just smiled. Angel tried to ask him another question and he placed his fingers to her lips.

'Shush, my child, it's OK,' he whispered.

She nodded, her whole body numb with shock still trying to get her head around the news.

It seemed the person responsible for Linda had been found after reports of another crime and that person's fingerprints matched the ones found on some clothing Linda was wearing at the time of her death.

'I should be getting back to the ward now, Dad, the nurses will think I've done a runner.' He nodded in agreement.

They both stood up and without saying another word, hugged each other goodbye and Angel walked off in the direction of the hospital main entrance and didn't look back trying to keep the tears inside. Up on the ward, she pulled the curtains around the bed and sat there crying. Half of her wanted to scream in anger and half of her wanted to curl up and die. She knew there was nothing she could do to fix the nightmare and that she had no choice but to deal with it. She heard the food trolleys and the noise of plates and cups being collected. It was the catering staff. A little petite lady looking very smart entered the bay she knew straight away no breakfast had been served to Angel.

'I see you have no empty crocks. 'Have you had any breakfast?'

Angel just glanced at her and shook her head.

'Would you like me to make you some toast and a cuppa?' she asked. 'Shouldn't really, but I won't tell if you don't,' she chuckled.

Angel nodded gracefully. The lady went off and was back within a few minutes armed with hot tea, steam escaping out of the top of the cup like a gurgling volcano, and just like cream to a cat, there Angel saw two pieces of hot buttered toast which smelt so divine, her taste buds doing the can, eagerly awaiting the first bite. Again Angel said nothing, just smiled as the sweet old lady put the plate and cup down on the table. The tea tasted sweet and a sharp bite which quenched her thirst.

'Come on, my little Daisy, eat up,' a soft voice said.

She looked up startled to see her mum standing at the end of the bed. She always called Angel, Daisy as long as she could remember and apart from Arthur, was the only person to do so. Angel had been in such a daze, she didn't hear the other patients' visitors coming nor realised the time.

'Mum,' she croaked.

'Yes, Daisy, I'm OK. Your dad came to see me earlier with some news,' she smiled.

'Yes, I know, he came to see me first,' she replied. 'Why are you smiling, Mum?' she asked puzzled.

Seems both Rosaleen and Arthur were relieved Angel was OK after everything that had happened and was glad she seemed to have closure on the awful news on the death of her best friend Linda.

A few days had since passed and Angel began to feel a lot better to the point she wanted to go home and put her life back together. So much had happened in a short space of time that being at the hospital was doing no good. She noticed Maxine was pottering about so called her over.

'Yes, my lovely, what can I do for you?' she asked.

'Erm, is it possible to discharge myself?' Angel asked.

Maxine looked puzzled and sat on the chair next to the bed. 'Is everything OK, hun?' she asked slightly concerned.

'I just want to go home, I'm fed up here,' Angel said feeling confident; there was no point beating about the bush.

'Can you go and ask for me please?' Is there a form I have to sign or something?' she asked eagerly.

'Give me a few minutes and I'll find out for you,' said Maxine with a look of confusion.

Angel got out of bed and began sorting her stuff, not that there was much, as her parents only brought in the minimum, thinking she would only be staying a couple of nights.

Maxine came back with a senior staff nurse who had a disapproving look as she approached the bed and what looked like a hospital file.

'Maxine informs me that you want to discharge yourself, is this correct?' she asked.

Angel nodded and just looked at her with a blank expression.

'Well, you do realize it's against medical advice,' she paused, sternly looked at Angel and continued, 'you've had a very nasty bang on the head and your tests are inconclusive at the moment.'

Angel scratched her forehead and tilted her head to one side.

'I just want to go home. If you have a problem with that then get me someone who doesn't, so I can just sign the bloody form and get out of this hellhole!'

She was beginning to get really irritated with the senior staff nurse and her sullen attitude. The nurse opened the file, took out a piece of paper, explained it was a disclaimer form and once signed, if anything happened, the hospital would not be liable in any way.

Angel signed the form without any hesitation. The nurse gave her a copy and she finished packing, made her way to the main corridor and realised she was too far from home to walk so called for a taxi. She sat on a bench by the lay-by waiting and noticed a little girl walking towards the car park with her mother. It reminded her of when she was little; Rosaleen and Angel would walk often to different places and talk as most little girls did with their mothers. The hospital entrance was so busy, cars coming and going, people busy walking to and from the hospital, getting on with different things. Angel started thinking about her parents and all what they had done for her over the years with going to school, college, university, her memories of sleep-overs with friends, and she wished she could turn back the clock. She decided to give them a call.

'Hello,' the voice said.

'Hi, Dad, I am on my way home. Can you call round later? I think we need to talk,' she asked feeling hopeful he would agree.

'I'll bring something for tea and cook,' he sounded chirpy and upbeat.

'OK, I look forward to it, see you later,' Angel cancelled the call, put her hands in her cardigan pockets and felt good that things were going to be OK.

The taxi pulled up, she got in and headed home. Once inside her apartment block, she wearily headed up the stairs because as per normal, the lift was out of order. She opened the apartment door and all that greeted her was silence. It sounded perfect. She slowly walked inside, dropped the bag in the hall and went straight into the kitchen and filled the kettle. Whilst waiting for it to boil, she wandered into the lounge and stood staring out of the window. She could see kids playing on the park and people walking their dogs a typical normal day, the trains whizzing past and the thunderous noise slightly echoing through the buildings. She let out a happy sigh, glad to be home, went back into the kitchen and poured water onto a herbal teabag, it smelt lovely and fruity. *Hmmm, just what I needed,* she thought.

Her mobile started ringing. She didn't care who it was and left it to go to voicemail and just went into her own little world in the lounge at the window watching the world go by, hot cup of tea hugged with both hands. A warm relaxed feeling started in the tips of her toes and worked its way up her body like sensual wave on a calm sea day.

Arthur had planned a special dinner, just him and Angel as they had done many times when she was younger, it was a sort of thing they had. She finished her tea and moments later there was a loud banging at the door that startled her. She froze on the spot and tried to ignore it. *Bang!* The door went again; it sounded like there was a herd of elephants on the other side. She placed the cup down and walked very slowly towards the door, looked through the spy hole and did not recognise the figure. It was a man but Angel didn't know him. She backed away quickly and hoped he would get fed up and go away; he did not and kept banging the door and shouting, calling out some really nasty names. After what seemed an eternity, she finally plucked up the courage to go to the door.

'Who are you?' she asked with a trembling voice.

'That's on need-to-know basis, and you do not need to know!' he grunted loudly.

His voice sounded cold and almost had an evil tone to it, and it sent a chill down her spine. Did he really think she was going to just open the door and let him in? Arthur was on his over to Angel's and noticed a male figure running out of the main door, so he hurried and made his way up to her apartment, knocked the door and seemed to panic. Angel let him in and told her dad of what happened. Arthur comforted his daughter and offered to stay the night but she declined. They had dinner as planned and Arthur left to return to the hotel him and Rosaleen were using on their stay in London.

Angel put the clean dishes away in the cupboard and decided to retreat to bed. She had a list of things to do in the morning which included ringing her boss and enquiring about the office. She switched off the lights in the kitchen and lounge, wandered into her bedroom and flopped on the bed, hugged it like a long lost friend she hadn't seen for a very long time. She woke up hours later, opened her eyes and looked around the room. Her senses were in overdrive and the hairs were moving on the back of her neck almost to the point of tickling her. The apartment was silent but a clicking noise could be heard clear as a bell. She listened intently trying to figure out what it was, tried to move and let out a big yelp, a huge soar of pain ripped through her body, warm liquid dribbling down her face! She knew she wasn't crying. She gritted her teeth through the pain to get up off the bed and hobbled to the lounge area clutching her side in agony, barely managing to flick the light switch on. She stood and froze in horror, the apartment door was moving, it hadn't shut properly when her dad left. Seems an uninvited visitor had popped by. Out of the silence, a horrible gruff voice kept saying her name slowly over and over again, hairs standing up all over her body in fear. Her phone was in the bedroom but no matter how hard she tried, she couldn't move. The voice sounded like it was getting closer. Was it still in the room with her?

She shut her eyes in the hope it was a nightmare and when she reopened her eyes, her worst nightmare was standing in front of her! The face she saw through the peephole not a few hours earlier was glaring at her no more than three feet away with evil wide eyes. Her throat tightened up and the fear took over, leaving her with the inability to scream. Her legs gave way under her as she fell the male figure cracked her over the head with a heavy blunt object. Angel flew across her laminate flooring with the force of the hit and lay helpless in a heap, blood pouring from her head all over her floor. The figure stood just looking over her, smiling with a vengeance. He was disturbed by a noise coming from the corridor and decided to leg it before he was seen... or so he thought.

Chapter 8

Arthur was back at the hospital. A doctor came over to have a chat with him.

'Hello, Mr Mayflower, my name is Dr Tawny. I am the leading consultant on the ICU ward,' he said.

'Erm, hello, erm, what's happening with my daughter?'

He wanted answers and fast, the person who saw the whole attack in the apartment had alerted the police and ambulance.

'Angel is in an induced coma to give her body chance to heal itself as she has suffered a lot of internal injuries in the attack,' his tone was sympathetic. Arthur couldn't believe what he was hearing; according to the witness, the male figure had been in the apartment since Angel had gone to bed, stood over her bed for a while just grinning, holding a shiny object.

'How serious is it?' he started to panic.

'In my professional opinion, I would call the rest of Angel's family and prepare yourselves for the worst,' he paused for a moment, 'I have to warn you, she may not last the night. The next 24 hours are critical,' he warned. Arthur wasted no time phoning around and getting everyone together to be at her bedside. A police officer came by to speak with Arthur. He gave the officer the facts on what had happened and who found Angel. He excused himself from the officer's presence and wanted to talk to Angel.

'Hello, my beautiful child,' a tear fell down his cheek 'it's your dad here. Come on, sweetheart, wake up, all the family is here waiting to speak to you, we all love you very much, Daisy-doo.' Arthur was tapped on the shoulder

'How is she, Uncle Arthur?' It was her Cousin Billy.

'Not too good, son,' Arthur sighed.

'They don't know whether she will survive the night.' Billy gasped in horror.

Angel's dad and cousin stood and hugged like they had never hugged before, both crying and praying for her survival.

Her Nanny Rose and Granddad came in moments later. All four of them were crying and saying anything they could think of to stay positive, but as the hours rolled on, it became increasingly harder and she was getting worse. The doctor had also told the family results for her MRI scan. The medical staff were hopeful as it showed brain activity, but her dad decided to go for a walk to stretch his legs. He only got as far as the corridor and burst into tears. Angry thoughts were coming into his head about this guy who had caused his daughter so much harm and as her dad, he wanted to get justice for his little girl as a way of making up for not being able to protect her. He felt so guilty for breaking the promise he made to Angel the day she was born that he would always be there no matter what and felt so guilty for not insisting on staying with her. He ventured down as far as the main entrance and just sat on a bench in disbelief. A woman sat down next to him.

'Are you OK?' she asked politely.

He stared at her kind face for a moment.

'No, erm, no, my, erm, daughter is in ICU and is very poorly,' he gulped hard to rid the lump developing in his throat but it was too late.

He buried his face in his hands and it became obvious to this lady he was heartbroken.

'I am really sorry to hear about your daughter. I hope she pulls through. My thoughts are with you.'

Arthur thanked her for the kind words and excused himself as it was time to go back up to the ward. Arthur was taking his time to return as he had lots of emotions to process. On arrival through the doors, there was a lot of commotion going on near to the bay. It wasn't until Arthur got closer he drastically realised the commotion was going on around Angel's bed! He saw her mom, Nan and cousin outside the relatives room and walked towards them.

'What the hell is happening?' he said panicking.

Her mom turned to him and could only whisper as she was trying so hard to keep the tears back and be strong.

'Angel is dying, Arthur. We have been asked to wait here for the doctor,' she wept.

The staff were working tirelessly to restart her heart, tubes all over her body, adrenaline pumped furiously into her veins. Angel was watching from above at the efforts of the staff and knew her time had come to an end. There was nothing she could do to reverse the decision that had been made for her, and after 50 minutes of endless CPR...

'Time of death, 13:07 pm,' the senior doctor called it.

Arthur was stood outside the resuscitation room and fell to his knees, hands in a clasp, and he shouted, 'NOOOOOOOOOOOOOOOOOOOOOOOOOOOOOO!'

The doctor made his way to the relatives room to break the news. He asked them all to be seated.

'I am very sorry to have to tell you, but we couldn't restart Angel's heart. Her injuries were too severe and we did everything we could to save her.'

The words felt like a concrete storm to her relatives and their hearts broke instantly. They all sat sobbing trying to digest the news that their little Daisy-doo had died.

A few days later, once her body had been released from the hospital morgue, Angel's family could get on with arranging the funeral. It was to be held in the local church in the town where she grew up as a child. She had been in a coma for fifty-three days, but had felt like hours to her family. They all said prayers at her bedside and read stories to her and sang songs. The nursing staff who looked after her said she may have been able to hear people. Angel's fragile petite body finally gave up in the hours of day fifty-four. Her soul was free to wander around and she was free of the awful pain she was in from the horrific attack. Steve, the guy who she met on the night out with Helen and Linda, was the male figure who tormented her with emails and texts, and who came to the apartment and beat her senseless and left her for dead. Why? He was jealous of the friendship between Angel and Linda. Helen, however, was part of his cunning plan, hence how he got hold of Angel's phone number, email address and apartment address. He wanted her out of the way, he succeeded. The person that reported him on that fateful night was Helen of all people! At the last minute, she wanted to back out but when she arrived at Angel's apartment, she realised she was too late as he'd already actioned his well-thought-out evil sadistic plan. She phoned the police and the ambulance in the severe hope he hadn't killed her friend. The reason behind it all was even though he had met Angel, they did not have a one-night stand, it was all her imagination. They did not get on very well at all and because she got very wary of him and had a bad feeling, she had warned Linda not to get involved, which lead Steve to putting Linda out of the picture, followed by Angel permanently. He was caught up with by police as they spotted him on their arrival hovering around the apartment building with a baseball bat that was dripping with blood.

Arthur had no idea Steve had been released on bail; had he known, Angel would've stayed with her parents at their hotel without a doubt. Her family decided on a colourful service with nobody being allowed to wear black. They wanted everyone to remember her in a positive way and celebrate her short-lived life the way she was. The order of service had a variety of readings and all the favourite songs she used to love instead of hymns. The whole community pulled together to prepare for the sad day. She was twenty-nine years old and had her whole life ahead, great career in the publishing sector, close-knit supportive family and a wonderful set of friends. The dreaded day finally arrived and Arthur had put her prime place at the front to see and hear everything said. Her family did her very proud, talking about the day she entered into the world and all the achievements right up until that fateful day thanks to Steve. Cousin Billy, who she hadn't seen very much due to his work commitments taking him abroad to live in Australia, read a very heartfelt speech about when they were kids and the silly playful pranks they used to play on each other, and how he so wished this too was a silly prank and that any minute the lid on her coffin would fly open and she would sit up and shout boo! He shed loads of tears whilst trying to remain calm for the sake of her father, who unlike her was very much alive. Arthur kept repeating to Rosaleen how parents shouldn't outlive their child and if he could swap places with Angel, he would do in a heartbeat. Nanny Rose and other close members of family also read similar speeches in their own words of her and what she meant to them and any little thing she had done or said that stuck out and made them laugh. After the lovely service, Angel was taken into the graveyard and given a burial to remember. All close family threw a red rose down onto the beautiful white coffin and said a last goodbye in their own way. Everyone was then invited back to Nan's house for a party. Family refused to call it a wake as it was a day of celebration, not sadness.

A few weeks later, the apartment she loved so much was sorted out and keys returned to the landlord who was so sad to hear his cheery tenant would never be coming back. Furniture and clothes were donated to charity. The end of an era. Angel held pride of place in her parents' home. They had a picture of her blown up to a big size, framed and hung above the fireplace.

Angel really missed being around family, not being able to talk to them, spend time with them, and most of all to just carry on being the joy she was – Angel Mayflower.

Amen